Join Mortimer Ant and all of his friends in getting out the word on the importance of reading.

Show your love of reading by flashing the symbol for "read" in sign language to your friends, family, or anyone you meet.

Simply make the shape of the letter "V" with your index finger and middle finger. Then move the "V" down the palm of your left hand.

Check out the little boy in the picture with Mortimer to see how it's done.

PUBLISHED BY PENTLAND PRESS, INC.
5122 Bur Oak Circle, Raleigh, North Carolina 27612
United States of America
919-782-0281

ISBN 1-57197-289-7
Library of Congress Control Number: 2001 130297

Printed in China

In *The Story of Mortimer Ant*, Connie and Jim McNab have used lyrical verse and bright, bold, whimsical illustrations to tell the tale of an ant and his picnic "antics."

What a delightful way to incorporate a rhythmic story with a valuable lesson about sharing and friendship. Readers both young and old will delight in this tale, and perhaps come up with a few "antics" of their own. ENJOY!

Valerie Welk
Kindergarten Teacher
Clovis Elementary School
Clovis Unified Schools
Clovis, California

Just about anyone who has ever been on a picnic has made acquaintance with an ant, or lots of ants. Ants and picnics seem to go together although, sad to say, most picnic partakers probably are not nearly so appreciative of their diminutive partners in picnicking, as is the boy in Jim McNab's wonderful poetic tale and Connie McNab's bright and happy illustrations. *The Story of Mortimer Ant* is, of course, a fantasy for children but it reminds us all that each species, no matter how small or occasionally pesky, occupies an important place in our world, which we all need to respect.

Cathy Critchley, Principal
Laton Elementary School
Laton, California

Author Jim McNab and illustrator Connie McNab live in Fletcher, North Carolina with their three dogs.

Jim, who is a captain for a major airline, has always had a love for writing and has used his talent to create a truly unique story.

Connie is a retired elementary teacher whose bright, bold colors make *The Story of Mortimer Ant* come alive!

Together, they hope you find as much joy in reading the book as they did in creating it.

Jim's Dedication

To my Grandmother, Idell McNab, who supported and
encouraged me from the beginning. To my 3rd grade
teacher, Mr. Philip Sciara, who prodded me and nurtured
my creativity. Finally, to my wife, Connie, whose love,
support, and inspiration is my motivation and drive.

Connie's Dedication

To my parents, Quinnylu and Ive Ridley and my stepmom
Rosalyn, thanks for being the greatest parents on earth. To my
niece, Jennifer Brooke Ridley, who is like a daughter to me and
I know will be the best kindergarten teacher ever! To my aunt,
Mary Helen Paulk, who inspired me to become a teacher. To
my best friend, Karen Bargamian, whose constant positive atti-
tude is always a reminder that I can do anything! And, last but
not least, to my husband Jim. Thanks for believing in me
enough to give me the opportunity to illustrate your first book.
I am truly honored!

There once was an ant named Mortimer
    Who had a very big family.
They lived in the ground and crawled all around
    In a place called an ant colony.

Mortimer had so many brothers and sisters
    He couldn't remember their names.
And there was always someone in Mortimer's family
    Who was ready to play some fun games.

The door Mortimer used to go outside his home
    Was a hole on top of the ground.
And during the day you could see Mortimer's friends
    All running around and around.

Mortimer the ant and all of his friends
    Liked to go play hide and seek.
They would play their game in the tall, tall grass
    Next to a small, winding creek.

There were many good places to hide from their pals
Behind the trees and the stones.
They would laugh and have a grand time
Until it was time to go home.

One day while playing their games
    A group of three people walked past.
They spread a blanket on top of the ground
    On top of the lush, green grass.

Mortimer Ant and all of his friends
    Had never in all of their life,
Seen the man over there who sat on the grass
    With his son and his lovely young wife.

The group of young ants peeked over a stump
    And wondered why the people were here.
Then they heard the man say to his wife,
    "What a great day for a picnic, my dear."

Mortimer came out from behind the old stump
     And was spotted by the couple's young son.
Mortimer was scared and wanted to leave
     But for some reason, he did not run.

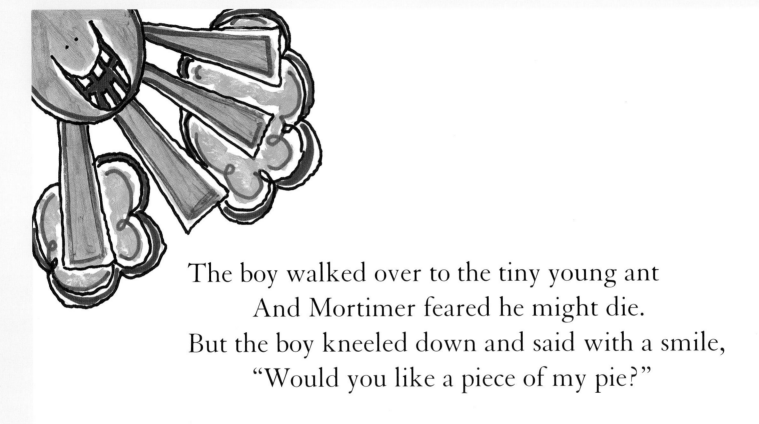

The boy walked over to the tiny young ant
And Mortimer feared he might die.
But the boy kneeled down and said with a smile,
"Would you like a piece of my pie?"

Mortimer said with a sigh of relief,
        "Thanks! That's so nice of you."
"I'm here with all of my friends.
        Is there enough for all of them too?"

The boy said, "Sure! Bring all of your friends.
We have plenty of food we can share.
We have all kinds of goodies to eat.
Please have a seat over there."

So, Mortimer the ant and all of his friends
        Sat there and had a big lunch.
By the smiles beaming from their little ant faces
        They sure were a happy young bunch.

The ants ended up having a sandwich
    Made of peanut butter and raspberry jelly.
They were so full that they lay on the ground
    And rubbed their stuffed, little bellies.

After they ate, the ants and the boy
  Played hide and seek for a while.
"Now it's your turn to run and go hide"
  Said Mortimer with a big smile.

Since the boy was much bigger than all of the ants,
He was really quite easy to find.
The boy so enjoyed playing the game
He really did not seem to mind.

The ants all had a wonderful day
    With the new friends they had just met.
But, now it was getting quite late.
    Gosh, it was almost sunset.

The ants all said, "Thanks so much for lunch.
        You have been so very kind."
The boy looked down and said to the ants,
        "You're welcome. Let's picnic again sometime."

The ants waved goodbye, and the boy said, "So long."
        Then they turned and they all walked away.
The ants went back to their hole in the ground,
        And told of their adventure that day.

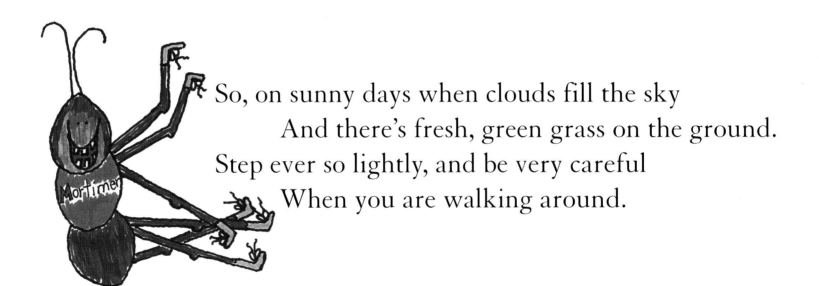

So, on sunny days when clouds fill the sky
 And there's fresh, green grass on the ground.
Step ever so lightly, and be very careful
 When you are walking around.

Mortimer ant and all of his friends
    May be there playing hide and seek.
If they are, make sure you ask
    If they'd all like something to eat.

After lunch, you'll have a great time
    Playing with the ants and their games.
But I'd be amazed if you can remember
    All of the ants and their names.

Just try to remember one, single name
Of the ant that you met here today.
The next time you see some ants on the ground,
"MORTIMER" is all you need say!